This book belongs to

In Blue's Shoes

The adventures of Blue, the super hero assistance dog

Story by Cindy Thoreson-Arnold and Laurie Brownell

Illustrations by Elizabeth Grace Hixon

This book honors assistance dogs of all types, shapes, and sizes
that are dedicated to helping individuals with disabilities.

Special thanks to Rochester Community Education Citizens Advisory Council, Hiawatha
Homes Foundation, Rochester Civitan Club, Pam Arnold-Greenwaldt, Terry Greenwaldt,
Andy Brownell, Jerry Brownell, and Can Do Canines Assistance Dogs

*Proceeds will benefit Hiawatha Homes Pet Therapy Program.

Printed by Johnson Printing
1416 Valleyhigh Drive NW, Rochester MN 55901

ISBN 978-0-615-91750-4

Blue Elf Publishing

Hello, my name is Blue.

I am a Can Do Canine.
I am bouncy, brave and true,
and there is nothing I can't do.

I can open the power door and
so much more!

I went to school to learn what to do.
I can pick up most anything – my paws
are as strong as glue.

I open doors and get the phone.
The best part is being rewarded with a bone.

I wear a cape that says working dog, please don't pet.

If you ask my owner Cindy, she will say yes...I bet.

My job is to help others and to be the very best.

Some days I take a break and get some well deserved rest.

I was helping Cindy in the grocery store.

I got a big surprise when I opened the freezer door.

Out popped an elf wearing pointy shoes and silly socks too.

She smiled and asked, "How do you do?"

"Very well," I say, "I am Blue, but who are you?"

"I'm Ellie, Santa's favorite elf at the North Pole.
I must be lost - I slipped and fell through a very big hole.
Can you help me find my way back to Santa's workshop?"

"Absolutely, I am a Can Do Canine and nothing can make me stop."

I lifted Ellie up into the air and we traveled up into space.
I realized that I had no idea of how to find this place.

We zoomed past stars, landing on a big round circle in the sky.
Uh – oh, I think we went too high.

Ellie quickly told me that this was not the spot.
So, down we flew with a quick shot.

It was dark and cold and we were surrounded by flying bats.
Their silly ears looked a lot like pointed hats.

"Is this the North Pole?"

I asked.

"This place is way too dark."
Ellie barked.

So, up and out we went.
We landed in a place with a very big tent.

We zoomed up and down,
and we sat in front of a clown with an upside down frown.

"Is this the North Pole?"

I asked.

"Wow, this place is too hilly!"
Ellie screamed.

We kept looking for Ellie's home as we soared through the sky.
All of a sudden we saw a reindeer pass by.

Follow that flashing nose Ellie advised.
So, we changed our direction and we were surprised!

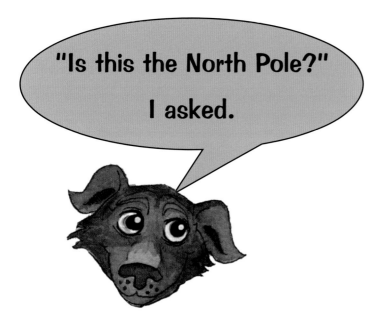

"Is this the North Pole?"

I asked.

"This is too windy to be my home!"
Ellie hollered.

We landed at the most
beautiful place.

And right then I saw the
happiest look on Ellie's face.

She ran to a jolly old man
with a long white beard and
a round tummy.

Ellie was finally home!

Everyone cheered and gave
us cookies, mmmm...
yummy.

Santa told everyone that I was a hero, we danced and threw confetti.
I heard Santa say that the big day was near and the elves must get ready.
I was the leader of their grand parade...
Suddenly my thoughts of Ellie and Santa began to fade.

Cindy woke me up and said it was
time to go to the grocery store.

She would need my help opening
the freezer door.

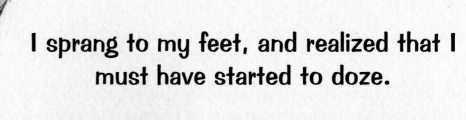

I sprang to my feet, and realized that I
must have started to doze.

She bent down and took a piece of
confetti off of my nose.

It's good to have a Can Do Canine
and super hero friend.

I will stand beside you
until the very end.

A helping paw I will lend.

It's good to have a Can-Do Canine
and a super hero for a friend.

Hiawatha Homes Foundation

Hiawatha Homes Foundation, is a private, non-profit 501c(3), that supports Hiawatha Homes, Inc. by accepting charitable contributions. The Hiawatha Homes Foundation Board of Directors manages these gifted funds and disburses them to meet the needs of people supported by Hiawatha Homes, Inc.

Hiawatha Homes Foundation also sponsors the annual Festival of Trees – A Celebration of Giving. This event benefits the work of Hiawatha Homes. The success of each year's Festival of Trees allows the Hiawatha Homes Foundation to give financial support to Hiawatha Homes, Inc. that makes a significant difference in the lives of the people we support. By supporting the Hiawatha Homes Foundation, your contribution supports the services offered by Hiawatha Homes, Inc. and the approximately 140 people in these programs. The support of the community is vital to the growth and quality of our work.

Hiawatha Home's Pet Therapy Program

Hello, our names are Fergie, Cassidy, and Val. We are very lucky to live in loving homes at Hiawatha Homes, Inc. Hiawatha Homes makes sure we are healthy and happy pets. They feed us, send us to training, take us to the doctor if we need shots or don't feel good, and always give us a special toy on our birthdays.

Our owners have disabilities and we help them with many things. We take them for walks to exercise, help them stretch their body by asking to be petted, and help them meet new people by being friendly.

Here are some skills I learned in school. I use them everyday to help Cindy with her activities of daily living and to help enhance her independence.

Open refrigerator

Retrieve phone

Retrieve keys

Open power door

When I'm not working
I enjoy relaxing and
having fun!

When you meet a service dog.....

Tips to follow when meeting or approaching a working service dog:

- Speak to the person first.

- Do not do anything to interrupt the assistance dog, such as making noises.

- Do not offer food to the service dog.

- Ask first to pet a service dog, only do so if the dog's owner has given you permission.

- Do not touch the service dog without asking for, and receiving, permission.

- Do not be upset if the dog's owner will not let you pet his or her dog.

- Offer help but do not insist.

- Never make assumptions about the individual's intelligence, feelings or abilities.

- Do not be afraid of the dog.

- When you meet a person with a service dog, please remember that the dog is working.

According to federal law, a service animal is not considered a pet. The Americans with Disabilities Act (ADA) gives people with disabilities the right to have their service animals in all areas open to the public. Service animal means any assistance dog or other animal trained to do work or perform tasks for an individual with a disability.
Source - pleasedontpetme.com and
workinglikedogs.com/resources/service dog etiquette

When You Meet a Person With A Disability...

· Be yourself when you meet a person with a disability.

· Remember that the person with a disability is a person first.

· Talk about the same things as you would with anyone else.

· Help the person only when they request it. Wait for the person to ask for help.

· Don't stop and stare when you see a person with a disability.

· Don't shower the person with kindness.

· Don't ask embarrassing questions.

· Be patient and don't offer pity or charity. The person with a disability wants to be treated like others.

· Enjoy your friendship with the person with a disability.

· Don't judge individuals with disabilities. You may find that you have the same interests.

· He or she is like anyone else except for the limitations of their disability.

· Don't be afraid to laugh with him/her.

Source: When Meeting a Person With a Disability - publication of
Courage Center of MN

Can Do Canines
ASSISTANCE DOGS

9440 Science Center Drive • New Hope, Minnesota 55428 • (763) 331.3000

Can Do Canines is dedicated to enhancing the quality of life for people with disabilities by creating beneficial partnerships with specially trained dogs. We envision a future in which every person who needs and wants an assistance dog can have one.

Our assistance dogs fetch amazing things! They provide the gifts of freedom, independence, and peace of mind to our clients and their families. Dogs, training, and supplies are provided to each client free of charge. Our fully trained dogs, often adopted from local animal shelters, are provided to individuals who live with disabilities.

Hearing Assist Dogs are often selected from local animal shelters. The dog alerts a person who is deaf or hard of hearing to sounds by making physical contact with them and then leading them to the source of the sound.

Mobility Assist Dogs work with people who have mobility challenges and other needs. They pick up and carry objects, pull wheelchairs, open doors, and help to pay at tall counters.

Diabetes Assist Dogs detect low blood sugar levels by sensing a change in their partner's breath. The dog alerts their partner by touching them in a significant way.

Seizure Response Dogs respond to a person having a seizure by licking their face, retrieving an emergency phone, and alerting other family members.

Autism Assist Dogs keep children with autism safe in public settings and help them experience the world more fully by offering comfort and assurance. These dogs serve as a social bridge between the family and the public.

Cindy Thoreson-Arnold and Blue

Blue and Cindy live in Byron MN. Can Do Canines Assistance Dogs brought Blue and Cindy together as a team in 2005. Blue is a rescue dog and is a Lab-Australian Shepherd. He is 10 ½ years old, and continues to be service dog, constant companion, and best friend.

Ellie is the goodwill ambassador for Hiawatha Home's Festival of Trees. She loves to go out and about in the community promoting the festival and shares her bubbly Christmas spirit with everyone she meets. Ellie always looks stunning, wearing her pointy shoes and silly socks too.

Laurie has been teaching disability awareness for over 25 years. She has collected children's books her whole life and always dreamed of writing a whimsical story to educate and entertain children of all ages. She lives in Rochester MN, with her husband and two children, who have enjoyed reading wacky children's books with their mom.

Elizabeth Grace Hixon is a graduate of the Minneapolis College of Art and Design. She now works as a freelance illustrator, painter and yoga instructor.